CAT PARADE

CAT PARADE

by Bethany Roberts
Illustrated by Diane Greenseid

CLARION BOOKS • New York

Clarion Books
a Houghton Mifflin Company imprint
215 Park Avenue South, New York, NY 10003
Text copyright © 1996 by Barbara Beverage
Illustrations copyright © 1996 by Diane Greenseid

The illustrations for this book were executed in gouache.
The text is set in 20/26-point Cantoria semi bold.

For information about this and other Houghton Mifflin trade and reference books
and multimedia products, visit The Bookstore at Houghton Mifflin
on the World Wide Web at (http://www.hmco.com/trade/).

Printed in the USA

Library of Congress Cataloging-in-Publication Data

Roberts, Bethany.
Cat parade! / by Bethany Roberts ; illustrated by Diane Greenseid.
p. cm.
Summary: The cat parade is enlivened by the arrival of a mouse.
ISBN 0-395-67893-5
[1. Cats—Fiction. 2. Mice—Fiction. 3. Parades—Fiction. 4. Stories in rhyme.]
I. Greenseid, Diane, ill. II. Title.
PZ8.3.R5295Cat 1996
[E]—dc20   93-26726
CIP
AC

WOZ 10 9 8 7 6 5 4 3 2 1

To Nina, with admiration and affection.

—*B.R.*

To Connie, Gail, Tom, Bob, and Pudrena, with love.

—*D.G.*

The cat parade comes up the street.
Rowr! Rowr! Rat-a-tat-tat!

Marching to a marching beat.
Tramp! Tramp! Rat-a-pat-pat!

"Down with mice! Up with cats!"
Rowr! Rowr! Rat-a-tat-tat!

Cats on floats. Cats in hats.
Tramp! Tramp! Rat-a-pat-pat!

**Closer, closer. Louder, LOUD!
ROWR! ROWR! RAT-A-TAT-TAT!**

Marching straight, marching proud.
TRAMP! TRAMP! RAT-A-PAT-PAT!

**Horns toot. Drums bash.
ROWR! ROWR! RAT-A-TAT-TAT!**

Tubas boom. Cymbals crash.
TRAMP! TRAMP! RAT-A-PAT-PAT!

**Balloons on tails. Siamese dance.
ROWR! ROWR! RAT-A-TAT-TAT!**

Bells on feet. Persians prance.
TRAMP! TRAMP! RAT-A-PAT-PAT!

Bugles blast. Trumpets bleat.
Rowr! Rowr! Rat-a-tat-tat!

Hundreds of cats on marching feet.
Tramp! Tramp! Rat-a-pat-pat!

Then, zip, nip. A mouse runs by.
Rowr! Rowr! Rat-a-tat-tat!

Drums scatter. Tubas fly.
Tramp! Tramp! "Catch that rat!"

Mouse hides in a dark, safe place.
Cats keep running. Pat-a-pat-pat!

The cats are gone. The mice can play.
Tubas! Drums! Rat-a-tat-tat!

"Up with mice! Down with cats!"
Tramp! Tramp! Rat-a-pat-pat!

Mice on floats. Mice in hats.
Squeak! Squeak! Rat-a-tat-tat!

Hundreds of mice come up the street.
Tramp! Tramp! Rat-a-pat-pat!

Marching to a marching beat.
Squeak! Squeak! Rat-a-tat-tat!